LEFT BEHIND

Clarion Books
a Houghton Mifflin Company imprint
215 Park Avenue South, New York, NY 10003
Text copyright © 1988 by Carol Carrick
Illustrations copyright © 1988 by Donald Carrick
For information about permission to reproduce
selections from this book, write to Permissions,
Houghton Mifflin Company, 2 Park Street, Boston, MA 02108
Printed in the USA

Library of Congress Cataloging-in-Publication Data
Carrick, Carol.
Left behind.

Summary: Christopher gets lost on the subway during
an excursion to the aquarium and is afraid he'll never
be reunited with his class.

[1. Lost children—Fiction]   I. Carrick, Donald,
ill.   II. Title.
PZ7.C2344Le 1988   [E]   88-1040
ISBN 0-89919-535-0   PA ISBN 0-395-54380-0

HOR 10 9 8 7 6 5 4 3

LEFT BEHIND

by CAROL CARRICK

pictures by DONALD CARRICK

Clarion Books
New York

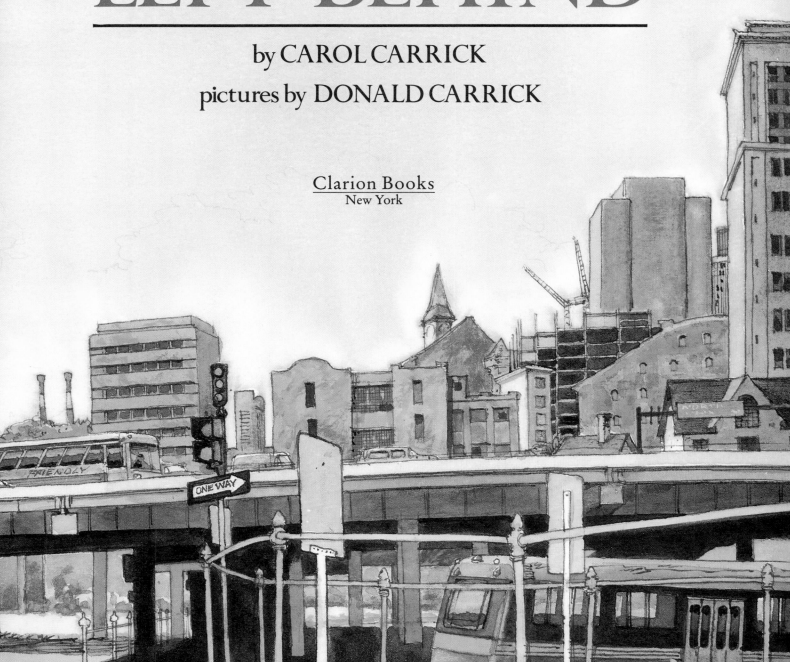

Christopher was excited when his class got on the bus to the city. Instead of going to school that day, they were going to the aquarium. He thought the best part would be when the bus dropped them off so they could ride on a subway.

Mrs. Snow was the leader of his group. She counted them before they went downstairs to the train. "Does everyone have a partner?" she asked.

Christopher grabbed Gray's hand. "I've got one."

Downstairs, Mrs. Snow put a token in the turn-stile as each of them went through. Christopher could hardly wait for the train to come. He had never been in the subway before. Why was it taking so long? Then from far down the track they heard a rumble. Headlights shone in the dark tunnel.

"It's coming," shouted the children.

The train roared into the station. It was so loud that Christopher held his hands over his ears.

As soon as the doors slid open, he started into the first car.

"Wait, wait!" said Mrs. Snow. "We all get on together."

Everyone took a partner's hand and climbed on.

"Can we look out the front of the car?" asked Christopher.

Mrs. Snow nodded. "But be sure to hold on."

The doors closed and the train moved out of the station into darkness.

Christopher and Gray pressed against the window, watching the signal lights change from red to green. The car rocked back and forth as they moved faster and faster. The brakes squealed around a sharp curve.

"Whoa!" Christopher yelled and he grabbed for a pole.

"Hold on," called Mrs. Snow.

When they got off the train, Mrs. Snow counted them again. "Take your partner's hand. Let's stay together," she said.

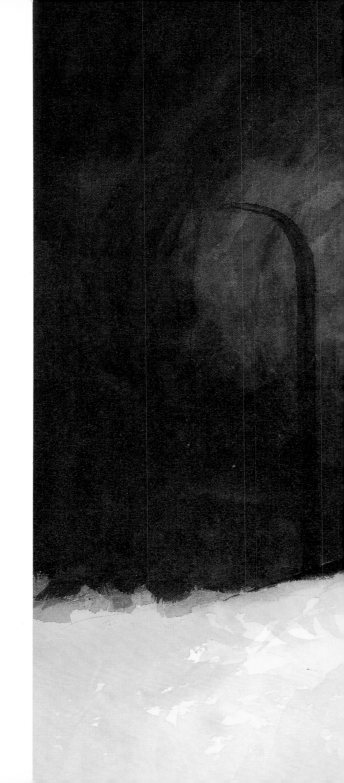

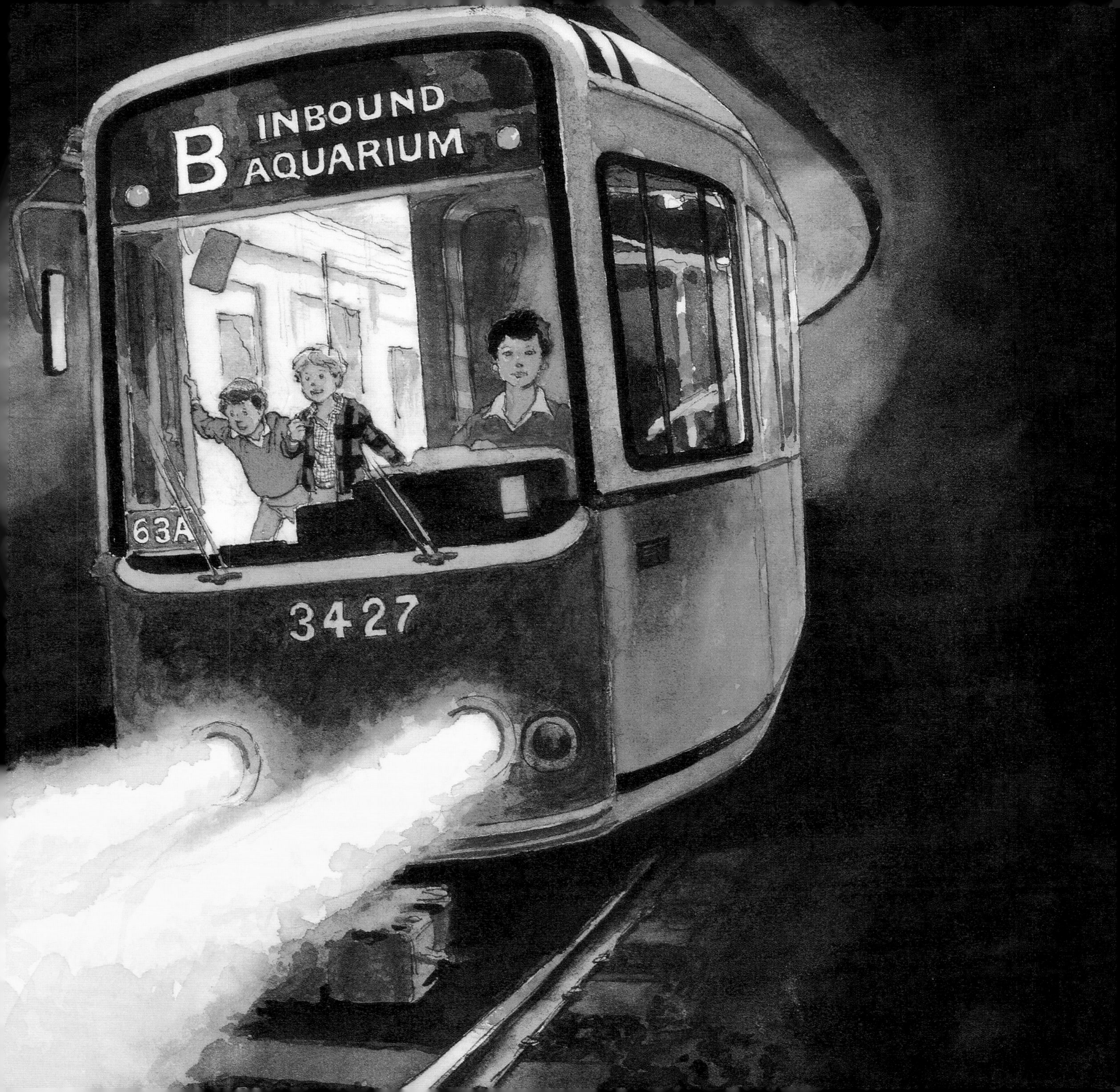

B
INBOUND
AQUARIUM
63A
3427

The aquarium was in a large building next to the harbor. While their teacher was buying tickets, Christopher peeked in at the big fish tank.

"Look," he said, running past the windows. "Turtles."

"Let's not get too far ahead, Christopher," Mrs. Snow called.

The class moved slowly from window to window, looking at big fish and little ones. But it was hard for Christopher to stay back with Gray; he was so excited.

Then it was time to go home. Christopher wanted to stand in the front of the first car again, but the train was too crowded. So he held onto a pole by the door.

Every time the train stopped, people pushed out and more people pushed on. Soon he was surrounded by strangers. He couldn't see anyone from his class, not even Gray.

The next time the train stopped, a crowd was waiting to get on. Behind Christopher, people were shoving toward the door.

"Let them off," someone called.

Christopher and the people around him stepped down onto the platform to let the others off.

The crowd on the platform pushed onto the train. Just as Christopher was about to get back on, a man squeezed in ahead of him. Before Christopher knew what was happening, the doors closed and the train was moving.

"Wait!"

Christopher started running, bumping into people along the platform. "Let me back on," he called, but the train didn't stop. Helplessly, he watched it disappear into the tunnel.

Christopher looked wildly around the platform. All he saw were strangers. How was he going to get home?

Another train came, and he panicked. Should he get on? He didn't know where it was going. He read the signs but none of them meant anything to him.

Christopher knew he had to get someone's help, so he went upstairs to find a policeman. He searched the station from one end to the other without seeing one. The smell from a donut stand was making him hungry. He looked in his pockets, but he didn't have enough money.

Maybe Mrs. Snow would come back for him.
He'd better wait where he had gotten off so she
could find him. Christopher went downstairs.
Was this the same platform? Now he was all
mixed up. If only he had stayed with Gray; then
he wouldn't be alone now. He tried hard not
to cry.

CROSSTOWN ⬆
INBOUND ⬇

A man in uniform came up to him. "What's the matter, kid?" he asked. "Are you lost?"

"I got off and the rest of them didn't," Christopher said.

"Do you know where you're supposed to be going?"

Christopher shook his head no.

The man talked to someone on his radio, and in a few minutes a policeman came. People stared as he wrote down Christopher's name and where he lived.

"How did you get lost?" the policeman wanted to know.

Christopher explained.

"Are you taking me home?" he asked.

The policeman said something he couldn't hear because another train was coming. Then they went to a waiting room in a different part of the station.

"Sit here," the policeman said.

"How will my teacher know where I am?" Christopher asked.

"We'll radio a call to every station. When we find her, we'll bring her here."

Christopher sat while the policeman talked to a man at the desk. He wondered how long it would be till the class noticed he was gone. He kept watching the clock on the wall. It seemed to take forever. Would Mrs. Snow be angry? And what about the other kids? He wiggled on the hard chair. They would think he was dumb.

After a long time he heard footsteps. "Mrs. Snow!"

She was coming down the hall with a policeman. Christopher jumped off his chair and ran to her. He was glad to see her even if she might be angry.

"I was scared you'd never find me," he said.

Mrs. Snow looked relieved. "I was scared, too."

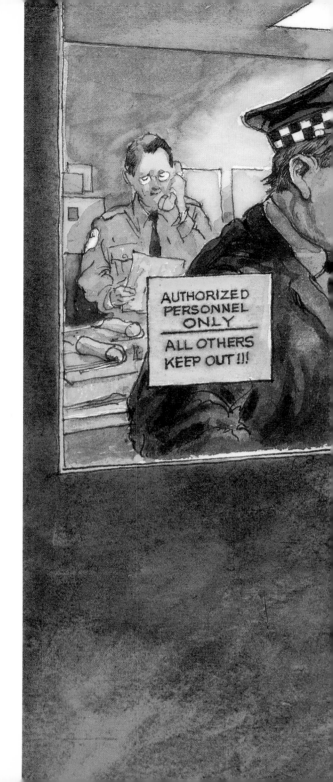

They said good-by to the policeman and went out on the
platform. A train was going by. Christopher thought the
people in the windows looked like fish in a tank.

"Everyone is waiting on the bus for us," said Mrs. Snow.

When their train came, Christopher was happy to take her
hand and get on it.